To Itty Bit, Teddy Bear, and Peanut.

—JTE

For my son Eddie, never stop dreaming.

—AJ

ZONDERKIDZ

A Christmas Gift for Santa
Copyright © 2019 by J. Theron Elkins
Illustrations © 2019 by Ag Jatkowska

Requests for information should be addressed to:

Zonderkidz, 3900 *Sparks Dr. SE, Grand Rapids, Michigan* 49546

Library of Congress Cataloging-in-Publication Data

Names: Elkins, J. Theron, author.
Title: A Christmas gift for Santa / by J. Theron Elkins.
Description: Grand Rapids, Michigan : Zonderkidz, [2019] | Summary: After a busy
    Christmas Eve, while his elves and reindeer sleep, a very tired Santa Claus looks
    to see if anyone left a present for him. |
Identifiers: LCCN 2019007035 (print) | LCCN 2019010229 (ebook) | ISBN
    9780310764441 () | ISBN 9780310729617 (hardcover) | ISBN 9780310764434
    (board book)
Subjects: | CYAC: Stories in rhyme. | Santa Claus--Fiction. | Gifts--Fiction. |
    Christmas--Fiction.
Classification: LCC PZ8.3.E444 (ebook) | LCC PZ8.3.E444 Chr 2019 (print) | DDC
    [E]--dc23

LC record available at https://lccn.loc.gov/2019007035

Art direction: Ron Huizinga

Printed in China

19 20 21 22 23 24 25 /DSC/ 20 19 18 17 16 15 14 13 12 11 10 9 8 7 6 5 4 3 2 1

A Christmas Gift for Santa
A Bedtime Book

Written by J. Theron Elkins

Illustrated by Ag Jatkowska

ZONDERkidz

In the cold North Pole
After Christmas night,
And a worldwide trip
On a reindeer flight,

Sat tired Santa Claus
In his brown leather chair,
In his old cottage house,
In his red underwear.

Just back from his travels
Where he left handmade toys
To be opened by all
Of the good girls and boys.
Would he get a present?
Santa quietly thought.
Did no one remember?
Was he simply forgot?

"Surely not," Santa said.
"There's a present for me.
I will search 'round this room
To find where it might be."

By the fire was his hat.
On the ledge was his suit.
Near the crèche was his pair
Of two old, buckled boots.

But no present was there...
There was no stocking stuffed
With candy or goodies
Or peppermint fluff.

His helpers were huddled
On the couch where they dozed
In polka-dot jammies
And jingle-belled toes.

But no present was there...
There was no paper bag
Stuffed with color tissue
And ribbon zigzags.

His reindeer were snuggled
At the base of the tree,
Snoring carols of Christmas
As content as can be.

But no present was there...
There was no box and bow
With bright shiny paper
From the twinkle lights' glow.

Then at last! By the bed,
Near the light, was a note.
In the note, were the words
That Mrs. Claus wrote.

Merry Christmas, my dear.
I am so proud of you!
I love you so much
And adore what you do!

Reading this, he just smiled
With a heart full of bliss.
Then he raised mistletoe
And he gave her a kiss!

"My love, here's your present,"
Thoughtful Mrs. Claus said.
"It was made from my heart
And was made for your head."

Santa's face looked excited
As he tore off the wrap...
And discovered his present
Was a knitted night cap!

"Oh, thank you!" said Santa.
"I was not forgot.
This night cap is jolly
And a wonderful thought."

After saying his thanks,
Santa said a short prayer.
Then he slid into bed
And he reached for his bear.

As his eyes slowly closed,
Once he turned off the light,
Santa whispered at last,
"Merry Christmas, sleep tight."